W9-AUI-638

A ROOKIE READER®

EVERYBODY SAYS

By Bonnie Dobkin

Illustrated by Keith Neely

Prepared under the direction of Robert Hillerich, Ph.D.

CHILDRENS PRESS®

CHICAGO

To Jeff, my Bear, who knew
these books would happen.

Library of Congress Cataloging-in-Publication Data

Dobkin, Bonnie.
   Everybody says / by Bonnie Dobkin ; illustrated by
Keith Neely.
     p. cm. — (A Rookie reader)
   Summary: A boy proud of his individuality
proclaims his love of raw broccoli, rainy days, and his
pet iguana.
   ISBN 0-516-02019-6
   [1. Individuality—Fiction.] I. Neely, Keith, 1943-
ill. II. Title. III. Series.
PZ7.D656Ev   1993
[E]—dc20   93-7835
                                    CIP
                                      AC

Everybody says
your shirt should match your pants.　3

I don't see why.

Everybody says
vegetables are awful.

But I love raw carrots.

Everybody says
cats and dogs make the best pets.

But I like my pet Iggy.

Everybody says
rainy days are boring.

I don't think so.

Everybody says
sports are the greatest.

But I'd rather read and draw.

Everybody says
collecting cards is cool.

I think keychains are cooler.

Everybody says
stuffed animals are for little kids.

But I still love Bumblebear.

Everybody says
it's more fun at the mall.

25

But I like to watch the ducks.

I guess I'm not everybody.

I guess I'm just me.
And do you know what?

I'm glad!

WORD LIST

and	don't	know	see
animals	draw	like	shirt
are	ducks	little	should
at	everybody	love	so
awful	for	make	sports
best	fun	mall	still
boring	glad	match	stuffed
Bumblebear	greatest	me	the
but	guess	more	think
cards	I	my	to
carrots	I'd	not	vegetables
cats	Iggy	pants	watch
collecting	I'm	pet(s)	what
cool	is	rainy	why
cooler	it's	rather	you
days	just	raw	your
do	keychains	read	
dogs	kids	says	

About the Author

Bonnie Dobkin grew up with the last name Bierman in Morton Grove, Illinois. She attended Maine East High School and later received a degree in education from the University of Illinois. A high-school teacher for several years, Bonnie eventually moved into educational publishing and now works as an executive editor. She lives in Arlington Heights, Illinois.

For story ideas, Bonnie relies on her three sons, Bryan, Michael, and Kevin; her husband Jeff, a dentist; and Kelsey, a confused dog of extremely mixed heritage. When not writing, Bonnie focuses on her other interests—music, community theatre, and chocolate.

About the Artist

Keith Neely attended the School of the Art Institute of Chicago and received a Bachelor of Fine Arts degree with honors from the Art Center College of Design, where he majored in illustration. He has worked as an art director, designer, and illustrator and has taught advertising illustration and advertising design at Biola College in La Mirada, California. Mr. Neely is currently a freelance illustrator whose work has appeared in numerous magazines, books, and advertisements. He lives in Los Osos, California, with his wife and five children.